THE GATEWAY

THE ATLAS OF CURSED PLACES

THE GATEWAY

KATHRYN J. BEHERNS

darbycreek

MINNEAPOLIS

Darby Creek
A division of Lerner Publishing Group, Inc.
241 First Avenue North
Minneapolis, MN 55401 USA

For reading levels and more information, look up this title at www.lernerbooks.com.

The images in this book is used with the permission of: © iStockphoto.com/Ainis (forest); © iStockphoto.com/Itus (woman); © iStockphoto.com/mustafahacalaki (skull); © iStockphoto.com/Igor Zhuravlov (storm); © iStockphoto.com/desifoto (graph paper); © iStockphoto.com/Trifonenko (blue flame); © iStockphoto.com/Anita Stizzoli (dark clouds).

Main body text set in Janson Text LT Std 12/17.5.
Typeface provided by Adobe Systems.

Library of Congress Cataloging-in-Publication Data

The Cataloging-in-Publication Data for *The Gateway* is on file at the Library of Congress.
ISBN 978-1-5124-1325-0 (lib. bdg.)
ISBN 978-1-5124-1353-3 (pbk.)
ISBN 978-1-5124-1354-0 (EB pdf)

Manufactured in the United States of America
1-39784-21322-3/29/2016

To all of my former students

CHAPTER 1

Mia and Hannah sprinted down the hall, slid around the corner, and reached the Earth Science classroom. Too late. The last bell of the morning rang out. Tardy for their very first class of their sophomore year. This year was off to a rough start.

They entered the room hoping Mr. Crapsnik wouldn't notice. Of course he did.

"So glad you could join us." He talked like he was pinching his nose. "Take a seat, ladies." His nasally voice continued, "Sooooo like I was saying. Our Big Bog was born about two and a half billion years ago. Today you will be going to the library to research the biodiversity, or living things, that call this bog home. Alright, peoples, let's go to the library." Mr. Crapsnik was your typical science nerd: high-waisted corduroys and a sweater vest—tucked in.

Mia and Hannah were the last ones to leave the classroom. Then, all of a sudden: *Thump-scrape! Thump-scrape! Thump-scrape!* Strange footsteps echoed from somewhere behind them. Mia and Hannah froze mid-step. Mia gasped as she turned to find her other best friend, Jasmine, almost nose-to-nose with her.

Jasmine could hardly breathe she was laughing so hard. "Got you! You were totally about to crap yourself!" Jasmine said. She was wearing heavy black boots with awkward heels. She looked very different from last year, when she'd mostly worn sweatshirts and jeans. She had dark makeup on around her green-brown eyes. Jewelry on her wrists. High heels to make her look even taller.

"I thought I was gonna be mugged by bigfoot," Hannah said, grinning at her friend. She'd missed Jasmine over the summer. Hannah, Mia, and Jasmine were usually inseparable, but this summer Jasmine had left Mia and Hannah to stay at her cousin's lake cabin.

"I thought I was going to have to lay the smack down." Smiling, Hannah wrapped her arms around Jasmine. "We missed you, lady. Where were you this morning? Knocked on your door, but no one answered. I think this might be the first time in like eight years we haven't walked together on the first day of school."

"Sorry, *Mom*. It will never happen again."

"It's just that we've been walking to school together since like second grade," said Hannah. "It felt weird. Like, *wrong*."

The hall was empty. Everybody else in Mr. Crapsnik's class was already at the library. But Mia, Hannah, and Jasmine weren't ready to break up their reunion for studying just yet. "Bathroom break, girls!" announced Hannah.

The girls' restroom had three primary purposes: 1) The obvious 2) a place to escape the outside world 3) a gathering space for gossiping and catching up. Some of the school's most important conversations took place among the white porcelain thrones. Hannah, Mia, and Jasmine migrated to the restroom.

"I missed you guys sooo much," Jasmine said, putting her arms around her friends. "But this summer was kind of good for me. Even being away from you two. It's like I got to try on someone else's life. And I liked it." She was trying so hard to make them understand. "I met new people, tried things. My cousin took me places. She showed me how to dress and do makeup. I like looking good. And that's good. I feel like I grew up more. Ya know what I mean?"

Hannah was distracted by the jangling sound of Jasmine's thin, gold bracelets. "Uh-huh."

"I know this sounds stupid, but I was actually scared to tell you that the reason I didn't walk with you this morning was because I'd just finished doing my hair and I didn't want it to frizz," Jasmine confessed.

Mia laughed a little. "Don't be silly. I don't care if you decided to gain four hundred pounds to become a sumo wrestler. You're our friend."

"Thanks, Mia," said Jasmine. "So, notice anything else different about me?"

"Your wrists jingle?" Hannah said.

"No, silly! I pierced my ears. Don't die of a heart attack or anything!" Jasmine wanted to take the words back as soon as they left her mouth.

Mia had had one of the worst summers of her life. Her grandma had died suddenly of heart problems. The grandma who baked her cookies every first day of school and would come to every basketball game, even when Mia's parents weren't there. Mia's eyes pooled with tears.

Hannah grabbed Mia's hand quick for a comforting squeeze, as if to say, "Everything is going to be okay."

"Oh crap. I'm sorry, Mia," Jasmine said. "That was bad—really bad."

"I'm fine," Mia said, trying to hold back her tears. "It's just still kind of hard. I saw her the night before the three-on-three tournament. Then Grammy just never woke up. I didn't get to say how much I loved her, or what she meant to me." Mia's voice started to crack. "I just want to say good-bye."

"I thought you didn't enter the tournament this year," said Jasmine, who now had her hand on her friend's shoulder in a gesture of sympathy.

Jasmine, Hannah, and Mia had dominated the tournament for two years.

"We couldn't this summer." Hannah could feel the anger rise up. "*Remember?* You were busy trying on 'a new life.'"

"We volunteered," Mia said, very quietly.

Hannah had been at the tournament when Mia got the news about her grandma's death. She was there to catch Mia when she fell apart between games. She was there all summer to help put Mia back together. Through it all, Mia and Hannah grew even closer.

"I'm sorry, Mia." Jasmine felt a little like the odd girl out. She wished she could find the right words to make Mia feel better.

"There you are!" Suddenly a fourth voice entered their conversation as Jayden from their

Earth Science class came into the bathroom. "Mr. Craps-Himself is starting to notice that some 'peoples' are missing. You better get back before he figures out who." Then, she glanced down at Jasmine's boots. "Nice."

"Thanks."

CHAPTER 2

"Be sure to pick your group for the field trip *before* you leave this library," Mr. Crapsnik droned just as Mia, Hannah, and Jasmine snuck in. They were trying to blend in by some magazine racks.

"You will be responsible for your safety and getting the assignment done. You will be graded on both."

The library smelled of old books, dust, and stale coffee. The librarian, Miss Jones, looked like she had been around since the dinosaurs. She always had a mug of coffee in her hand as if it were attached to her body. "You girls look like you're searching for something very important. Can I help you?" she asked Mia, Hannah, and Jasmine.

"Ummmm, yeah," Jasmine said, relieved the librarian wasn't busting them for being late. "We're looking for information on the Big Bog."

Miss Jones was a small woman with crystal blue eyes that seemed to be hiding something. "I have the book you *must* read. It holds the bog's truths." She stepped so close the girls could feel her hot, coffee breath on them. She whispered as if possessed, "Beware of the jeweler's son!"

Then she backed away. "The book you are looking for is in the old part of the library through that door. It will be the one you bang your knee on." She was pointing toward an arched door that had lions carved into its wood.

"Did you ever notice that door?" asked Mia.

"Never," replied Hannah. "It's like it showed up out of nowhere."

"I think you *and* Miss Jones have lost your marbles," Jasmine said.

No one saw the girls walk through the arched doorway. They entered an eerily silent room filled with rows and rows of ancient books. These books were titled things like *Conjuring Magic from the Earth* and *Potions for Everyday Living.*

Mia ran her fingers down the rows of old books until she came across one that stuck out about four inches past the bookshelf. Miss Jones was right; she would have hit the book with her knee. The cover was scratched. Its corners were rounded from use. It was blood red with gold letters: *The Atlas of Cursed Places.* Mia wiped the dust off and lifted the cover. The first page of the book was a map with skulls on it. Suddenly, the pages began to turn themselves. Page after page whirred by, finally stopping at a chapter: "The Big Bog: Gateway to Death and Life."

"Whoa! This just got real!" Hannah said. Goosebumps popped up on her arms.

"It sounds like something an old lady with too much time on her hands made up." Jasmine didn't take her eyes off her phone.

Had she even seen the pages turn themselves?

Mia and Hannah sat at the only table in the room. They could hear their classmates in the main library, but they sounded a whole world away.

"Are you reading this, Mia?" Hannah asked. "It says here that in the 1800s a woman named Melanie Zurner went for a walk by the Big Bog. Witnesses said she was wearing what looked like a wedding dress. She was never seen again. Two hundred years later, no body has been recovered. She was lured through the gateway into the land of the dead." This sounded more like fiction than like something found in any atlas.

They continued reading:

The bog is but a gateway between the world of the living and the land of the dead. At twilight the living and the dead merge and unite. Say these words and the Gateway opens, "Death to life you must cross through. Into the Gateway we summon you." In your hand provide an object the deceased person once held dear.

"Do you believe this, Mia?" asked Hannah.

"I don't know," replied Mia. *I want to*, she thought. She was gripping her grandma's butterfly clip that she had kept in her pocket since the funeral. What she wouldn't give to say, "I love you" one last time. To truly say good-bye to her grandma. She wondered if Grandma would still smell of strawberries and fabric softener.

"You don't actually believe this crap," Jasmine said, looking up from her screen. "It sounds like a practical joke if you ask me."

"Well, what's the worst thing that could happen?" replied Hannah. "We get muddy."

They looked over at Jasmine who had completely checked out while she stared at her screen.

Mia leaned into Hannah so that Jasmine wouldn't hear. "I have to do this, Hannah."

"Tonight, at twilight," Hannah whispered.

"Why are you whispering?" asked Jasmine.

"Didn't want to disturb you while you were on your phone," said Mia. She meant it as a dig, but after a few seconds Jasmine just shrugged and went back to her cell. Mia picked up the ancient book and slid it into her backpack. "I have a lot of research to do tonight," she whispered to Hannah, the friend who actually cared about her.

CHAPTER 3

Mia came running into Hannah's house. "Sorry I'm late! Jasmine wouldn't leave me alone. She kept wanting to hang out."

Hannah looked up at the clock. "Crap! We can take my mom's car. She's working late, and my brother is at football practice."

"If you think it's a good idea." Mia was nervous. Hannah only had a provisional license. One driving ticket would ruin her chance of getting her driver's license any time soon.

"Otherwise we won't get out there in time. We don't have a choice."

They hopped into the silver minivan. Hannah anxiously adjusted the mirrors and checked her seatbelt. Then she adjusted the mirrors again.

"Um, don't mean to rush you, but I think the sun is going to be down any second," Mia said.

Hannah backed the car out of the driveway, then popped it into drive. "You want fast, you've got it!" Still, Hannah's "fast" was just a little speedier than an elderly driver's.

They drove beyond the neat and tidy rows of houses in town. The road followed an old creek that used to be mined for iron ore. The ore gave the water a red tinge. They were driving slightly downhill until finally the creek disappeared into a large clump of trees. The sun was starting to set behind them.

Hannah parked and Mia leaped out of the car and ran for the row of pine trees that surrounded the bog like a giant fence. Hannah trailed close behind.

The ground beneath them was soft like a hollow grave. A huge blackbird cawed its warning at them. Locusts buzzed and frogs croaked loudly.

Strange-looking plants grew at the edge of the bog. Trees stuck out of the bog. Their branches seemed to be reaching out for help before they drowned in the bog's acidic water.

"Are you ready, Mia?" Hannah asked.

Mia held Grandma's butterfly clip out to the bog like she was giving it to someone.

"Death to life you must cross through. Into the Gateway we summon you." Mia chanted it over and over again, saying it louder each time.

The sun dropped behind the horizon, where the earth met the sky. The animals and bugs went silent. The sky turned a bright shade of purple. Hannah and Mia had never seen a color like that.

The bog, which had just seconds ago been lapping at their feet, began to bubble. It burped and belched up sulfur-smelling air, as if hell were breathing on them. Mia trembled, clip in hand. She wanted her grandma back more than anything, more than life or death, heaven or hell.

Then in the distance, across the bog, a figure appeared. Mia saw it first. The figure—a woman—walked on top of the bog's boiling surface.

"It's Grammy," Mia shouted. Fear shot through her. What if Grammy was no longer in a form she recognized? What if she was a zombie? What had they done?

The figure got closer. Hannah and Mia could see it was not Grammy at all. She was young and tall, with dark hair. This strange woman continued walking—no, running— toward them. She was tripping and stumbled over the bubbling water, but she kept coming.

Hannah stepped back, never turning her eyes from the figure coming for them. "Oh God! She's mad. A-a-and she's coming right for us."

"No, no." Mia was strangely calm. "She looks desperate, maybe even scared. Definitely not mad."

The two girls had no time to call out to her or to run. Before they could do anything, she was gone.

Stunned, silent, Mia and Hannah looked out over the bog. Its bubbles and belches had stopped. The smell lingered, but there was no sign of the woman in the bog.

"Was that real?" asked Hannah.

"I think so," replied Mia. "What did she want?"

"I don't know. Something important, based on the way she was running."

They turned to head back to the car. Getting to the row of trees, they saw another dark-haired figure approaching. This one was very much alive and angry.

"Who do you think you are, ditching me like that? I thought we were best friends. I thought we did everything together! You didn't even ask me to come with you." Jasmine sounded really hurt. "I knew something was up when you had that stuck-up smile in the library. You couldn't *wait* to get rid of me after school, could you, Mia?"

"I just figured you wouldn't want to come out here."

"How did you know where to find us?" asked Hannah.

"Let's just say I had a hunch. Besides, it's not that far." Jasmine was trying hard not to yell anymore. "Oh, and nice car, Hannah! I'm sure your mom would love to hear how you *stole* it!"

Hannah got scared and said, "Jasmine, don't. I would be grounded for life. Don't tell her PLEASE!"

"Whatever. I'm not a snitch."

"You want a ride back to town?" asked Hannah.

"No. I'd rather bike home than be with you traitors." Jasmine looked as though she were about to cry. She turned and started walking toward the bog.

"Should we stop her?" whispered Mia.

"She'll be fine. I don't think she will be summoning any ghosts," said Hannah. "Besides, she needs some space."

Mia walked around the back of the car to get into the passenger seat.

"Look," Mia said, pointing to the rear window.

"That's strange," said Hannah. "There's writing on the window . . . and it's backwards."

They got in the car. Looked in their rearview mirror. The words had been written in mud: *Beware of the jeweler's son*.

"That was what Miss Jones said to us in the library," said Mia.

"Jasmine must have written it."

"I guess. But why?"

"Probably to spook us," replied Hannah.

"It worked," Mia said. She had the eerie feeling that someone was watching them.

CHAPTER 4

"Now class," Mr. Crapsnik said. He had a cold so he sounded even *more* nasally than usual. "We are going to embark on our first field trip. Remember to get with the buddies you picked last week." He looked over at Mia, Hannah, and Jasmine. "And stick together." Even Mr. Crapsnik could tell there was trouble in paradise.

"Man, things really can change in a week," Mia said under her breath.

The class waited for the bus in the cool fall air. Everyone boarded when it arrived. Hannah sat next to Jasmine, who was by the window. Mia was across the aisle from them.

"So," Hannah said, trying to make the best of the situation. "I haven't seen you around much."

"I've been super busy," Jasmine replied. "Spirit Week is going to be so much fun!"

Jasmine was on the homecoming committee. Homecoming was only two and a half weeks away. She was in charge of Spirit Week, which took place the entire week of homecoming. That week was always packed with all kinds of fun events. Teachers even wore school colors and gave out less homework.

"So what crazy things do you have planned?" asked Mia as she leaned over the aisle of the bus to talk to Jasmine.

"Oh, you know, the usual," Jasmine said coldly.

"No I don't know," said Hannah. "Why don't you tell us?"

"I promised the senior class president I wouldn't. She's in charge of the whole thing. Wouldn't want to let down a good friend. Hmmm?"

"You don't have to be mean about it, Jasmine," Hannah said. "We're still friends. We even tried to sit with you at lunch yesterday—"

"But there wasn't room to sit by me because I have *other* friends," Jasmine interrupted.

"Keep it down now, kids. We're just arriving at the Big Bog. I want to go through some rules." Mr. Crapsnik talked about staying with your buddies, completing the bog scavenger hunt activity—the purpose of that day's field trip—and not going to the caves on the other side of the bog. He pointed to a shadowy area with no trees. "It is completely *off* limits. There are dangerous sinkholes. You will fail if you fall in a sinkhole."

Mia, Hannah, and Jasmine got off the bus. Jasmine grabbed the activity instructions and stormed off.

"Jasmine, wait!" Mia chased after her.

She stopped and turned to Mia, now just a few feet behind. "Stop following me! I don't want your friendship. I don't need it. You can take your little three-on-three tourneys and secret trips to the bog and shove it! I'll find new friends." She turned around and walked away.

CHAPTER 5

Mia could feel a lump form in her throat. It felt like she was losing another person she loved. She swallowed her sadness down.

"She's just angry," Hannah said as she caught up to Mia. "You know Jasmine. She doesn't think before she speaks."

"Yeah. I guess I just miss the way things used to be."

"Me, too." Hannah felt heavy. "Sometimes growing up sucks."

Mia knew exactly what she meant. After losing Grammy, and now this, she felt like life was really kicking her butt.

They walked silently to the bog's edge.

"I guess we better look at our assignment," said Mia. "What's first on the list?"

"Woman walking across the bog," said Hannah.

The color left Mia's face. "You can't be serious."

Hannah could hardly keep a straight face. "Peat moss. That's first."

They looked up over the bog. Green and red fuzz coated the mucky water.

Mia started to laugh at how obvious the first item was to find. "I hope the entire list is like this. We'll be napping on the bus in no time."

"Let's look for some of these animals," said Hannah. "Northern Leopard Frog. See any?"

"Yuck. No, thank God."

The edge of the bog was slippery with greasy mud. A blackbird cawed. The birds that had been singing earlier that morning fell silent. The bog sucked up any sound around them into its mossy carpet.

Mia couldn't shake the feeling that something was about to happen. As if all life around the bog was holding its breath.

She screamed.

"What?" yelped Hannah.

Mia was pointing and flailing around. "Your legs!"

Hannah had eight slimy amphibians stuck to them. A ninth one crawled up her shoe.

"Salamanders!" Hannah carefully picked each one off of her pant legs. "I used to find these things under our deck when I was like six." She held the last one up so she could make eye contact with it. "Aren't they cute?" She turned it toward Mia.

Mia squealed and leaped back. "Disgusting. At least it's one less slimy thing for us to find. Now on to more nastiness."

"I hear some frogs over there. Come on. Follow me."

"Can't wait."

Mia let Hannah lead the way.

Above the girls, the sky shifted, as if someone had pulled a dull purple curtain over its blueness. Hannah and Mia were looking down: Hannah looking for frogs and Mia trying to avoid frogs. They didn't notice how far they were from the rest of their classmates.

"Hannah! Look at this." Mia had found a pitcher-shaped plant filled with water. Floating in the water was the decaying flesh of a baby bunny. Its eyeballs gone, fur dissolved. All that was left were threads of gray muscle and pearly-white bone.

Hannah groaned. "That's the pitcher plant on our list. It can eat insects and small animals."

"I didn't realize how big a small animal actually was." Mia was crouching down. "Look at the poor little guy."

They continued walking around the bog.

"Plants can eat animals," Mia said warily.

"I guess, and salamanders can attack humans."

"And dead people talk to the living!" said Mia.

"Only at the bog," said Hannah.

They both tried to laugh even though it was more unnerving than funny.

"Frog!" Hannah reached for it. The frog leapt forward. Hannah slipped and landed in the mire. Greasy mud soaked through the knees of her jeans. They ran after the frog, not noticing how far they had gotten from the bus and the others. Every time they got close enough to grab the frog, it would leap out of their grasp.

"He's too quick," Mia said. She looked up. They were almost at the opposite side of the bog. She noticed the purple sky, which reminded her of the evening when she saw the woman walking across the bog. "I think maybe we should turn back, Hannah."

"Now? No way!" Hannah was all in. Her hair was stringy with mud; her shoes were weighed down by clumps of mud; her clothes looked like she had been mud wrestling. "I am going to catch a frog if it's the last thing I do!"

There were frogs bouncing everywhere. Hannah took off after them. It brought back memories of when she used go frog hunting with her dad as a little girl. She started to laugh while she chased them. She dodged tree branches and bushes as she ran. There had to be at least a hundred now, all leaping in the same direction, and all just out of Hannah's reach. They came to a clearing where the frogs instantly scattered in different directions. Hannah looked up. Mia had caught up to her.

They were in the shadowy area of the bog. It was like a natural graveyard, without the headstones. Small mounds covered with feathery grass looked like new graves, while the sinkholes looked like the dead had escaped. Hannah and Mia carefully wound their way around the many sinkholes. They tried to stay on mounds that felt like sponges beneath their feet.

There was a flash of gold in a large crack on the side of a mound that Hannah was standing on.

"Check this out."

"What is it?" asked Mia.

Hannah bent down low. It was perfectly round and smooth with some sort of a chain. "It looks like a locket or something." It was hard to tell what it was because it was covered in mud.

Hannah reached for it with her whole body, her tippy toes the only anchor keeping her from face-planting into the mud. She was almost touching the metal object when the ground slid beneath her feet. The mound collapsed into the earth, making another sinkhole.

"I got it!" Hannah cried from inside the sinkhole. "Look at this." Despite the mound collapsing, Hannah still managed to grab the shiny object. "Mia! Check it out—a pocket watch."

Mia couldn't. She was transfixed by the gray, lifeless hand sticking out of the newly exposed dirt. She couldn't speak. She couldn't move. She could only look at the stiff icy hand that seemed to reach out to them. It was delicate with thin fingers and nails that looked like they had at one time been well kept. It was attached to an equally lifeless body.

By now Hannah realized there was something wrong—very wrong. "Mia, what is it?" Turning around, Hannah screamed. The body lay inches away. Hannah scrambled out of the sinkhole.

"She looks like she's sleeping," Mia said. "Look at the dress." It was an underdress.

"Who cares what she's wearing," said Hannah. "I almost touched a dead person."

Maybe it was because Mia had just lost her grandma or maybe it was morbid curiosity, but she began to scan the dead woman. Looking for anything that might tell Mia who she was or where she came from. "She's missing an earring." Mia was right. Underneath the body's long hair, she had only one emerald earring in her left ear.

Hannah couldn't look at the body. She was trying desperately to pretend it wasn't there. "This pocket watch . . . it has an inscription on it. *In every jewel lives a memory. May you have as many memories as I have jewels, my son. Your loving father, S.E. Trefare.*"

But Mia wasn't listening. She was deep in thought. "Do you think it's the Zurner woman the atlas talked about?"

Hannah was trying not to feel anything, which was almost impossible. "Listen, Mia. If we don't get out of here now and tell someone, I'm going to have a nervous breakdown."

CHAPTER 6

By the time they reached Mr. Crapsnik and the rest of their class, they were out of breath. Mr. Crapsnik had to ask the girls to slow down. "Take deep breaths."

"Body . . . bog . . . in the bog . . . a hand . . . cold . . . the frog led us there," Hannah stuttered.

Mia had to take over. "There is a body sticking out of the mud in the bog. Over there!" She pointed to the shadowy, forbidden area. Then she added, "I know we weren't supposed to go over there. Please don't fail us." All Mr. Crapsnik did was grab his phone and start dialing.

Within minutes, police arrived. They were able to carefully exhume the body and clear off most of the mud.

"When you examine the body," the detective said to another officer, "it looks like it has only been dead for a few hours. But if you consider where the body was located and how much sediment had built up around her, you'd think she'd been there for a good two hundred years." He scratched his head. "Plus, we haven't had a missing persons report in years."

The coroner put the deceased woman into a black bag. Mia could see all of her now. She once again noticed the earring in the woman's left ear. A small vine of gold ivy and delicate emerald leaves that wove their way down the side of the mysterious woman's earlobe. Despite the trauma the woman may have gone through, that tiny earring still had a little sparkle to it.

"She's missing her right earring," said Mia.

"By golly, it *is* missing. Well that sort of thing is bound to happen when a person is busy dying." The detective didn't even look at Mia or Hannah while he spoke. He checked his cell phone and moved away.

"Don't worry, ladies," Mr. Crapsnik offered in a reassuring voice. "Everything will be okay."

"Thanks," Hannah said. It wasn't like Mr. Crapsnik to be so nice.

He nodded. "Don't worry about your grade on today's project either. Turning up a missing person is more than I expected *anyone* to do on our class scavenger hunt."

The students started boarding the bus. Mia and Hannah took a seat in the back. Jasmine hadn't gotten on yet.

"Can you believe what just happened?" said Hannah.

"I know," said Mia. "And I can't stop thinking about that woman running towards us when we went to the bog for the first time. The woman had long, dark hair. She even wore a white flowy dress kind of like the one on the body."

"Do you think it's the same person?" Hannah asked.

"I . . . I think it has to be," said Mia, sounding more certain now. Suddenly, she could feel it deep inside her. "It was like everything kept leading us toward her body," Mia said.

"Maybe we just helped a ghost finally find some peace," replied Hannah.

They sat quietly in the peace of knowing they had brought closure to not just the ghost, but potentially to the family of that dead person. Perhaps some good could come from tragedy.

The bus started up and began to lurch forward.

"Wait!" shouted Hannah. "Where's Jasmine?"

She stood up, looking quickly through the rows of seats. Not one student on the bus had Jasmine's long dark hair. "Mr. Crapsnik! Jasmine. Where's Jasmine?"

CHAPTER 7

Mr. Crapsnik ripped the phone he'd been using away from his ear. "Stop the bus! Everyone stay seated. You and you"—he pointed to Mia and Hannah—"come with me."

They split up, yelling Jasmine's name. A few minutes later, Jasmine and a boy came sheepishly marching out of the trees. They clearly had been doing more than just completing the scavenger hunt activity Mr. Crapsnik had assigned.

"Jasmine!" Mia hugged her. It had been such a weird day. She couldn't have handled losing Jasmine.

"You are in big trouble!" Hannah led Jasmine and the boy onto the bus. "Just sit down and act like you have been here the whole time."

"Mr. Crapsnik!" shouted Hannah. "I'm sorry. I was wrong. Jasmine is on the bus. She was just sleeping."

Mr. Crapsnik turned bright red. "It has been a *very* big day. It's probably a good idea for all of us to sit still and be silent." Wisps of hair bounced as he talked. He kind of looked like a young Albert Einstein, except for the bald spot on the top of his pointy head.

"Who's that?" Hannah asked, glancing at the boy next to Jasmine as she walked by.

"Eddy," replied Jasmine. She was definitely trying to show him off; after all, he was tall, muscular, and had big brown eyes that seemed to look right through a person. "He's a *friend* of mine."

"He's a bit more than a friend, I'd say," Mia said quietly, trying not to let Eddy hear.

Jasmine replied loudly enough for Eddy to hear easily. "He knows the bog like the back of his hand. He's amazing. I just followed him around and we got Mr. Crapsnik's activity done within minutes." She turned to the young man who was staring blankly out window. "You are so smart." She put her hand on his knee.

"You go to school here?" Hannah asked Eddy suspiciously.

"Yep." He didn't even turn to look at her.

"Why haven't I seen you before?" Hannah did not like this guy.

Jasmine answered for him. "He goes to our school," Jasmine chimed in. "I can't help it if you're too stuck up to notice him."

"Oh, come on. All you think about is yourself and how you look." Hannah remembered the first day of school when Jasmine wore those bracelets and how she had carried on about how "gorge" they were.

"Jealous much? You just can't get over the fact that I don't need you or Mia."

Eddy had turned to look at Hannah and Mia now. He had a smile on his face, almost like seeing the three of them bicker gave him pleasure.

"Alright, kids! Sit down! Everyone just be quiet for a while!" Mr. Crapsnik looked like he was about to pass out.

Hannah glared at Eddy, then turned and walked to the back of the bus. Mia followed. She paused and said to Jasmine, "I'm just worried about you, Jasmine."

"Well don't be! I know what I'm doing."

Behind Jasmine's back, Eddy winked at Hannah. Then his dark eyes narrowed. His stare burned into Hannah. She had a flash of fear pulse through her, like the moment you wake from a nightmare then realize it was only a dream.

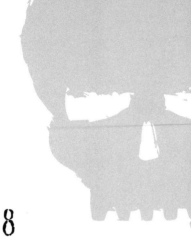

CHAPTER 8

"No, Principal Mock," said Jasmine, "you are *not* doing the Stanky Leg."

"Are you sure? 'Cause I can make my leg look like rubber." He started wobbling his legs. "How about the Nay Nay? I've been working on it for a while now." His arms started flailing. He looked like one of those floppy air dancers outside the used-car dealership.

Jasmine had to bite her lip so she wouldn't burst out laughing. "I'm sorry, Mr. Mock. That won't be necessary. We're going to be sticking with the original choreography from Michael Jackson's "Thriller."

"I see. Well I can get crunk with that." He was kind of shaking his head as he made air pistols with his hands. "This principal knows how to get his freak on." He pretend-shot into the wall behind Jasmine.

"Great!" The laughter was rising up inside of her. "I can't stay. Keep on practicing the dance clip I sent you." She darted to the nearest bathroom to burst out laughing. Then she immediately thought, *I have to tell Hannah and Mia*. It was out of habit.

For the past few days, Jasmine had been hard at work solidifying last-minute Spirit Week plans. Each day had a different activity. Monday it was Backwards Day. Tuesday was Pajama Day. Wednesday was Twins Day, when couples and good friends would come to school dressed alike. Thursday was Costume Day, where students would dress up like anyone but themselves. Finally, on Friday, everyone was supposed to wear green and black to show school pride at the pep rally.

Jasmine had planned a flash mob at the rally. She'd been secretly working with teachers, the principal, staff, and few students. Hence the hilarious moment with Principal Mock and many more awkward interactions with other adults. It was all a great distraction up until now.

After eating every lunch together, walking to and from school together, and especially meeting in the girls' bathroom to talk, it was dawning on Jasmine that it was all over. It was almost like her friends had disappeared— except worse. Hannah and Mia were still buddy-buddy. They kept doing the "friends" stuff. It was kind of like a part of her was missing. The bathroom's empty, echo-y silence made Jasmine's loneliness cut deep. Still, she did have Eddy. He was very sweet, not to mention handsome. And he was waiting for her at the main entrance.

CHAPTER 9

"Jasmine, don't think so hard," said Eddy as he snuck up behind her and kissed her on the cheek. "It looks painful. What are we working on today?"

For the past week Eddy had dedicated himself to whatever Jasmine needed, from stealing sticky notes from the English teacher to giving Jasmine a gentle shoulder rub at lunch.

They stood near the main entrance. She leaned into him and gave him a squeeze. "We've just got these signs to hang, and I need to finish the banner . . ." Jasmine's words trailed off as she smelled something gross.

It smelled like mud and fish guts rotting. At first she didn't want to say anything, but as Eddy put his arm around her, the smell got stronger.

"Do you smell that?" she asked. She started looking around.

"I don't smell anything," said Eddy.

Jasmine moved away from him, not wanting to make it too obvious. The stench faded.

Jasmine handed him the tape and signs and said, "We're going to split up." It wasn't just that he smelled; there was a job to be done. "You go and hang these signs in the freshman hallway. I'll be in the junior hallway getting things ready."

Jasmine climbed the stairs. A burst of cold air ran shivers down her spine. Then it was gone.

She reached the top and walked down the long hallway lined with gray lockers. The only people in the building besides Jasmine and Eddy were the principal and the custodians. Because she was on the homecoming committee, she had special permission to be there later than other students. She also had access to some of the custodians' closets. They were like little dank dungeons with the smell of chemicals and rotting things.

Jasmine walked over to one of the closets and grabbed the banner she had been storing in there, as well as a handful of paintbrushes. The banner had the words "Spirit Week" outlined in pencil. Now she needed to paint it. She unrolled the banner to see how it looked, expecting to find her words stenciled on the paper. Instead she found a huge a scribbled image of what resembled a pocket watch with its circular body, chain, and clock face. The image was sloppily drawn using brown greasy sludge that smelled like something rotten. She went back into the closet to see if she had just grabbed the wrong banner, but it was the only one there. Her heart pounded; her jaw clenched.

Who would have done something like this? Why would they draw a pocket watch with mud? Jasmine couldn't make a connection. Nonetheless, she had so much work to do. Now that she was starting over with the banner, taking time to think about what had just happened was not an option.

Jasmine took out a roll of tape and some signs she had printed earlier in the day. She started hanging them up. The lights were dim. All doors were locked. Jasmine hung a sign by the stairs and continued to walk down the silent, empty hallway. She took a step and behind her she heard the shuffle of another set of feet. She whipped around to see who it was.

No one.

She quickly hung up another sign and walked on. The shuffling was louder this time.

"This isn't funny, Eddy!" she said.

No answer. She started walking again. The footsteps sounded so close she could touch the person.

Jasmine spun around in the empty hallway. "Eddy! Stop it!"

Again, no one, but when Jasmine exhaled she saw the foggy puff of her breath, as if she were outside in the winter.

She ran toward the stairs. Toward Eddy who was still in the freshman hallway.

As she got closer to Eddy, the lights went out. The hall had no windows. Even the emergency lights were out. Total blackness enveloped her.

Jasmine couldn't see the walls beside her, let alone her feet below her. She tripped over a doorstop, landing on the tile floor. She could feel a warm breath near her ear. She screamed. The breath whispered something. It seemed like a warning. "Beware . . ." But Jasmine couldn't make out the rest of the words. She fumbled in the blackness to get up. Feeling her way along the lockers, she made it to the stairs. As she descended, she could see the distant glow of the freshman hallway.

Eddy was busy rolling tape to stick to the back of the homecoming signs. He already had one side of the hallway covered in Spirit Week signs. He clearly had been busy while she was upstairs.

Jasmine was shaking. She was still in shock.

"What's wrong, babe?" Eddy asked.

Worried that Eddy would think she was a nut job, Jasmine said, "This is going to sound crazy, but someone drew a pocket watch on the banner in mud. I mean who does that? And a pocket watch of all things!"

"Do you think someone is playing a joke on you? Mia and Hannah aren't your friends anymore. Maybe they did it." He gently enveloped her in a hug. "Come on now. Everything is okay. I'm sure there's a logical reason for it all."

His words were reassuring, but his body language wasn't. He looked on edge.

"Whoever it was, or *whatever* it was, just made a whole lot more work for me to do this weekend."

Scooping up her backpack and the rest of the signs, Eddy said, "We can finish it together this weekend. Let's get out of here."

The lights flickered as Jasmine and Eddy left the school. Jasmine couldn't seem to lose the feeling that someone was near.

CHAPTER 10

Sunday afternoon Jasmine's doorbell rang. She ran to the door—stomach fluttering, palms sweating, her mind racing. Eddy had never come to her house. Hopefully he wouldn't judge her based on the home her parents bought as a fixer-upper but never got around to fixing up.

She opened the door. Eddy stood with a bouquet of flowers he had picked on his way to see her. "These are for you, my lovely flower."

Jasmine took the flowers. The whole thing was a little over the top for two people meeting up on a Sunday afternoon to finish a banner. Still, it was very sweet.

Jasmine led him to her room where a clean banner, brushes, and paint waited. She had already started to sketch the words and the school's mascot, a phantom, onto the banner.

"Incredible job, Jasmine," Eddy said as he moved closer to Jasmine. "You are very talented."

"It's really not a big deal. I just stenciled some letters and drew a ghost."

"I'm not just talking about the banner," Eddy said. "The whole week—you planned it all." Eddy scooted closer as he spoke.

"I had some help." She winked at him.

"Some, but not from Mia and Hannah. Some friends they are. They didn't even check to see if you needed anything. I'm just glad I'm here . . ." He put his hand on hers. "With you."

Jasmine blushed. "I'm glad you're here, too."

Eddy put his hand in his pocket and pulled out a delicate earring. "I've been meaning to give this to you, but I just couldn't seem to find the right time. Until now." He brushed a piece of her dark hair out of her face.

Looking down at the gift she said, "It's beautiful! Thank you so much."

"It's sort of an heirloom. This earring belonged to someone very dear to me. Unfortunately, I can't find the other earring."

"It's beautiful," Jasmine said again. She grabbed his face and gave him a kiss. She turned her head to take out her old earring and slip the new one into her ear. "I guess we had better get to work, huh?"

Eddy started to kiss Jasmine again and again. "It has been so long, Jasmine. Such a long wait." He was moving his hands along her side.

Jasmine was not ready for this. She really liked Eddy. He was very sweet, but this seemed a little too quick. "Come on, Eddy. We really need to get this done."

He was softly kissing her neck.

"I really don't want to do this right now. I—" She felt uncomfortable and tried to sit up a little. "Eddy, let's get our work done . . . The committee is counting on me . . ." But the more she spoke and tried to sit up, the more forceful and pushy Eddy got.

Eddy was almost on top of her now. He reached the edge of her pants, feeling for the button.

"Eddy! Stop!" Jasmine pushed him off of her and sat up. "I think it's time for you to go."

Eddy glared at Jasmine as if he absolutely hated her guts. He towered over Jasmine. Fear flashed through her. She quickly scurried off the bed and away from him.

Then, as if a switch shut off, he was fine. Smiling, as if nothing had happened. "You're probably right. I should have known better." He gave a sweet bow, as if he were an 1800s gentleman, and walked out of the room.

CHAPTER 11

It was a gray Monday with rain spitting down from the sky. Hannah and Mia walked to school in their pajamas. On Friday, Eddy had reminded them to wear their pajamas for Spirit Week.

While walking they met a classmate wearing his backpack on his chest, then other students with their jackets on backwards. As they got closer to the school, they saw more and more people who had their clothes on backwards. Some were even walking backwards.

"Has the world started spinning backwards? I thought it was Pajama Day." Mia looked a little like a drowned Cookie Monster in her blue, rain-soaked footie pajamas.

"Great! Just great." Hannah was so angry her face had turned the same color as her matching red footie pajamas. "Eddy lied about what day it is! He made us look like morons."

The entrance to the school was covered in a shimmer of black and green streamers. The homecoming banner, which Jasmine had managed to finish, looked like it was written in emeralds.

Mia and Hannah entered the school. People stared at them. Some even pointed and laughed. They did the walk of shame down the hall to their lockers.

Their lockers were right next to Jasmine's. The three girls picked the lockers the year before, when they were best friends. Back then they would share ChapStick and class notes. Now Jasmine stood there talking and giggling with Eddy. Most of the time she pretended Mia and Hannah didn't exist.

Jasmine and Eddy had already talked about what happened in Jasmine's room the other day.

He apologized over and over again. Jasmine decided to forgive him. He'd been so sweet up until that moment. It had to have been a mistake. Jasmine and Eddy were now laughing and having a wild thumb-wrestling match.

Mia stepped right between Jasmine and Eddy. "What did we ever do to you?"

"That was low!" Hannah squeezed the side of her hips. She was trying hard not to grab Eddy's shirt. She had an older brother and could hold her own in a fight. Besides, this kind of sleazeball would probably have no problem swinging at a girl. "I suppose you're in on it too, huh, Jasmine?"

"I don't even know what you're talking about." Jasmine stepped away from Eddy.

"Your prince charming, here, lied to us on Friday. He said today was Pajama Day," Hannah told Jasmine.

"He totally made us look like fools. I know we don't talk anymore, but I didn't know you hated us." Mia sounded more hurt than angry.

"Look," Eddy stepped in and put his arm around Jasmine, as if to say that he owned her now. "This is one big misunderstanding. You must have heard me wrong because I would have never said that."

"I know what I heard," said Mia. "You did it on purpose."

"Sorry, guys. I must have gotten my days mixed up," Eddy said with an insincere smile. He turned to Jasmine and pulled her away, snickering under his breath.

"Did you really lie to them?" Jasmine asked after they were away from Mia and Hannah.

"Yeah, I was just messing with them. I thought you would think it was funny." He started to laugh when he thought about how ridiculous they looked. "Did you see them? Matching footie pajamas—which one is dumb and which one is dumber?"

Jasmine wasn't laughing. "That wasn't nice."

"Come on, baby. It was a harmless prank."

Jasmine was still silent. Eddy dropped to his knees in front of her. "Please forgive me, baby," he cried out dramatically, trying to make Jasmine smile. People in the hall gathered around, laughing at the whole scene.

Jasmine couldn't take it. She burst into laughter, too. "Alright, alright. Get up, you goofball."

"You have to admit, they looked pretty funny," said Eddy.

"Fine," Jasmine caved, "they did look a little funny but don't mess with them anymore."

"Aye, aye, captain," Eddy said as he saluted Jasmine. They entered their first-hour class with Mr. Crapsnik.

CHAPTER 12

The smell of formaldehyde was so strong Jasmine could taste it. Mr. Crapsnik wore his white lab coat and safety goggles.

"We have been discussing the friendly phylum *Annelida*. Today we are going to dissect our little invertebrate neighbor, the earthworm." Mr. Crapsnik held up the worm as if it were talking. In a high-pitched voice he said, "Howdy class! Please make sure you follow all the instructions and pick yourself out a nice, juicy, wormy friend."

"Mr. Crapsnik is one strange dude," whispered Mia.

"I can't tell if he's trying to be funny and failing at it, or if he really is that creepy." Hannah laughed under her breath.

Each pair of students filed to the back of the room with their dead worm and a bunch of tools that may or may not have been stolen from a condemned emergency room.

Eddy and Jasmine's lab station was across from Hannah and Mia's station. Jasmine turned to Mia and Hannah and whispered, "I'm sorry." She truly was, but Hannah and Mia both stared coldly at her. They were still wearing soggy footie pajamas.

Eddy nudged her and whispered, "Don't worry about it. They're fine. Help me slice this worm open. We need to pin him down."

Jasmine still really cared about Mia and Hannah, but there wasn't much she could do to prove it to them at the moment. She turned back to Eddy as he made a cut down the length of the worm's body. Jasmine felt a tap on her shoulder. She turned around.

No one.

The formaldehyde was starting to give Jasmine a headache.

"Can you hold this flap of skin on the worm while I go and get some pins to hold the body open?" Eddy asked.

"Sure." Jasmine tried to hide how much her hand was shaking as she held down the tiny flap of skin on the dead worm. Jasmine was terrified of creepy-crawly things, especially when they were dead.

She looked at the disgusting worm. One of its ends twitched, then the other. Jasmine blinked and rubbed her eyes. *I didn't just see that*, she thought. Then, as if possessed, the worm squirmed in an "S" pattern. Pieces of its guts fell off while it wiggled and rolled. Then it wrapped itself so tightly around Jasmine's fingers that it squished all of its insides into her hand and all over her fingers.

She screamed. Mr. Crapsnik ran to her. Hannah and Mia were there. Eddy was by her side now, too. They all looked down at Jasmine's hand. Part of the worm was in her hand, but most of it was smeared between the dissection tray and her fingers.

"I see you will need a new worm," Mr. Crapsnik said. He was so angry he was almost shaking. "Why did you do this, Jasmine? How? Never mind. I don't even want to know."

"The worm . . . it moved in my hand," Jasmine tried to explain. Seeing the disbelief on his face and even Eddy's, she gave up. "The formaldehyde fumes must be getting to me."

Mia and Hannah were very concerned, but they went back to their station. They knew how sometimes, in certain situations, the dead could come to life.

Jasmine put her head down on her desk. Suddenly she was burning up on the inside. She was even starting to break out in a sweat. But no sooner did she close her eyes to try to block out the world and give her mind a rest than the fire alarm began to sound.

All at once, the whole school was rushing to get outside. Once everyone was gathered on the lawn, Mr. Crapsnik found Eddy and

Jasmine. He pulled them aside and said, "Listen, I don't know what you two have been up to, but what just happened with the worm will not happen in my classroom. Jasmine, I am very disappointed in you. Screaming in the middle of class and squishing that worm. I just don't understand the pleasure in that." His voice was controlled, but just barely. Judging by the vein popping out of his forehead, it must have taken him every ounce of energy to not to yell in front of the entire shivering student body. "I will let this go, but you will never be lab partners again!"

Jasmine was shaking. She had no idea what had just happened. Mia and Hannah came over to her.

"Are you okay?" asked Hannah.

"I don't know." Jasmine was so confused. "Strange things have been happening to me over the past week." Jasmine started to tell about the footsteps in the junior hallway, the strange blackout, being tapped on the shoulder, even the feeling of being watched while she and Eddy were together.

Before Mia and Hannah could say anything, the fire alarm stopped. The all-clear was given.

The mob of students, teachers, and administrators slowly moved back into the school.

"Thanks for listening, you guys," Jasmine said. "It kind of felt like old times."

Hannah had a broad smile on her face. "I know. I've missed our talks." She gave Jasmine a hug. As Hannah pulled away she yelped, "Ow! Something's hooked."

Jasmine's earring had snagged some of Hannah's hair.

Jasmine took out the earring to detangle it from the clump of hair. "Eddy gave it to me." She held up the small string of emerald ivy. Mia and Hannah stared at the earring, speechless. The gems were the same size and shape as the one found on the body. There was a long, awkward silence between them.

"I guess I'll be going in now," Jasmine said. It was clear that Hannah and Mia didn't like that she was with Eddy.

After Jasmine had gone back inside, Mia said, "Are you wondering the same thing I am?"

"Where did Eddy get that earring?"

"Exactly." Mia was very concerned.

"And what about all the weird stuff that has been happening to Jasmine?"

"It all started after she met Eddy," said Mia.

Hannah nodded. "Eddy's the common thread. Should we say something?"

"I guess." Mia started to bite her nails. She knew Jasmine, and she knew where they stood when it came to Eddy. They were going to have to be *very* careful in how they talked to Jasmine. They were entering a minefield; one wrong word and they'd really blow their friendship to smithereens.

CHAPTER 13

Jasmine had been looking forward to Twins Day ever since Eddy agreed to dress like her. She had made a t-shirt for him with the words "Hands off! She's mine." On the bottom of the shirt was a handprint. She made herself an identical one that said, "Hands off! He's mine." Strutting down the hall to her locker, she was excited to show Eddy what she had made. As she got near, though, an awful, putrid smell met her.

Her eyes watered. She reached for her locker, gagging. Trying to hold her breath. The stench was unbearable. Lifting the handle, she swung open the locker door. Thousands and thousands of worms spilled from her locker. They were not the formaldehyde kind of worms she had dissected yesterday. These were worms that ate dead things and pooped dirt. They were covered in slime, knotting themselves together. Clumps fell to the ground, covering Jasmine's feet. The earthworms twisted and rolled around in a tangle of slime.

Giving a friendly wave from down the long hall, Hannah shouted, "Hey, Jasmine!"

Jasmine was too horrified to comprehend who was talking to her.

***

"Jasmine, Jasmine. It's Hannah and Mia."

Jasmine opened her eyes a little. She could see Mia and Hannah standing over her, holding her hand.

"You blacked out," said Mia. "Someone played a terrible practical joke on you."

Jasmine remembered. She winced at the thought of all those worms and that smell.

"Did you happen to grab the other t-shirt? It looks like this one except—"

Mia and Hannah shook their heads.

"Sorry," Mia said. "Didn't see it. We just had the school nurse come get you right away when you blacked out. You had to be carried away on a stretcher. You're in the nurse's office now."

"We actually want to talk to you about something right away," Hannah said. "I know this is super bad timing . . . but it's really important."

Jasmine was playing with the earring Eddy gave her as she lay in the nurse's office. The nurse was out for the moment making a phone call.

Mia was uneasy. "Now, I want you to have an open mind." She shifted in her chair. She wanted so badly to make Jasmine see what she saw in Eddy: a liar, a thief, and a jerk. "Hannah and I have been doing a lot of thinking about all of the strange things happening to you lately. We found one thing all of these events have in common."

"Really?"

"Eddy." Hannah started to talk faster because she could tell Jasmine didn't want to hear it. "He was around for every single event. He may not have been right there, but he was near. What if he is the one causing all of the hauntings?"

Jasmine cut her off. "That's ridiculous! There were so many times when he was there to help and comfort me. He's been nothing but amazing to me. He cares too much about me to do any of these things to me." Jasmine was now sitting up.

"Even the earring looks like the one missing from the body we found in the bog," Mia tried to explain.

"Oh that's just great! What did he do? Go and find the dead body and steal it from her? No way! You're crazy! Crazy jealous! You can't handle me being happy without you—"

Eddy rushed into the nurse's office just then. "Jasmine! Are you okay?" He gave her a big kiss. Then he turned to Mia and Hannah. "I can't believe you have the guts to come in here and stand next to Jasmine after what you did! Putting all those worms in her locker! You should be ashamed of yourselves!"

Hannah and Mia were shocked.

"No wonder you were blaming Eddy for all of the stuff that has been happening to me," said Jasmine. "It was you two all along!" Jasmine's anger turned to hurt. "Why would you do that? I thought we were friends. You know I'm terrified of that kind of stuff."

"We didn't do anything!" Hannah pleaded. "*He* is lying, Jasmine! We'd never do something like that."

"Yeah right! I saw you putting something in her locker." Eddy pointed while he shouted. "You're still mad about the Spirit Week mix-up, aren't you? Well, Jasmine had nothing to do with it." Eddy just kept on ranting so that Mia and Hannah couldn't talk over him. "You need to leave! Now! Get out of here!"

Mia and Hannah saw the principal coming toward the nurse's office. They left before things got even more out of hand.

They went back to the worm-filled locker. The custodians had taken care of most of the mess. It no longer smelled like something rotting. Now it just smelled like the pink barf powder they must have used to clean up all the slime. Hannah and Mia sat down at the end of the hallway.

"What was that all about?" asked Mia.

"I don't know, but Eddy is evil. He's lying to us. He's lying to Jasmine. All of these things that keep happening to Jasmine, they all have to do with Eddy. I know he has something to do with them!"

"I think so too, but what?" asked Mia.

"I have no idea. I think we should keep a close eye on him," replied Hannah.

"You're going to have to do better than that, ladies," Eddy was standing just around the corner from them. He crouched down and whispered, "Jasmine is mine. Soon you will never be able to change that. So keep your little eyes on me now, but soon we will be together forever." He turned and spoke directly to Hannah, "By the way, I think you have a little something of mine." He reached into the front pocket of her backpack and pulled out the pocket watch she found at the bog. Then he stood up and walked away.

"He's . . ." Hannah said.

Mia finished her sentence: "The jeweler's son."

"But how could that be? He'd be over two hundred years old."

"I don't know, but I think I know where to look for our answer." Mia had been carrying *The Atlas of Cursed Places* ever since that evening at the bog. She scanned the section about the Big Bog. "Read this," she said.

At dawn and twilight the Gateway shall open. The dead can pass through from the underworld to the living. But the dead can never again belong to the land of the living. They may only visit from sunup to sundown. If a soul outstays his welcome, and the sun sets completely, he shall die a soul's death and no more of him will remain.

"So Eddy's . . ." Mia said.

This time Hannah finished *her* sentence: "Eddy's dead-y."

They both shuddered at the thought.

CHAPTER 14

The pep rally was only a day away. Jasmine didn't want to think about what had happened yesterday, but her brain kept going back to it. Back to what Eddy had said. Then she would think back to what Mia and Hannah said. She didn't know what to believe. She didn't know whom to trust anymore. But for now, Jasmine had to get busy. There were lots of things that needed to get done before Friday. She threw herself into the work.

Throughout the day, before school and between classes, she busied herself with pep-rally preparations. Now it was the end of the day.

Microphone—the final thing on her to-do list. She needed to find a microphone. It was a pretty simple task: track down a custodian. Except Jasmine couldn't find a custodian anywhere. It was as though all the custodians had left the building at the same time. She found herself walking up and down halls, climbing staircase after staircase. No souls in sight. She walked down a small hallway just off the auditorium.

"Excuse me, miss. Miss!" Jasmine saw a woman turn the corner. "Please, wait! I just need—" Jasmine followed her. "Miss, please stop! I just need a microphone for the pep rally tomorrow."

The woman stopped and turned around. She was wearing a flowing nightgown and had long dark hair.

Jasmine was surprised by her appearance. Most custodians didn't dress up for Spirit Week. "You have the best ghost costume I have ever seen. Go Phantoms!"

The woman motioned for Jasmine to follow. She walked quickly, almost floating, through back doors and secret halls. Yes, Jasmine had been given permission to enter rooms and areas that were otherwise off-limits. But who knew there were all these tunnels? The woman occasionally glanced over her shoulder to make sure Jasmine was still following. Then she rushed on. The hurried unlatching of doors and noisy clanking of keys echoed down the hallways and corridors. Then silence.

Jasmine hurried down a gray hall. At the end of it there was a large room with its doors flung wide open. It was as though the doors were inviting Jasmine to enter.

"Hello? Are you in here?"

The windowless room was empty.

Jasmine saw a microphone sitting on a work table. She went over and grabbed it. Just beneath was the match to her emerald ivy earring. Jasmine turned the earring over in her hand, wondering what all of this meant. Then she felt a cool breath on her neck. "Beware of the jeweler's son," a voice hissed. Its warm breath smelled of death and decay.

Jasmine spun around to see who it was.

No one.

A chill ran down her spine. She didn't know if she was more scared of the figure that seemed to have disappeared into the air or the fact that Eddy was somehow involved.

CHAPTER 15

It was finally Friday, the day Jasmine had
been planning for and looking forward to
for weeks—but after the incident with the
microphone, all Jasmine could feel was scared.
Fear of what may happen next consumed her.
And her heart ached over her troubles with
her friends. Her heard broke for the boy she'd
trusted. Yet still Jasmine was convinced that
the show must go on.

Over the last couple of weeks, she had
taught all of the teachers, the marching band,
and choir members the dance routine for
the flash mob, but it was hard to trust that
everyone would be where they were supposed

to be and that they all would know the routine. Jasmine would introduce the principal. Then Eddy would start the music. The principal would start dancing. The teachers on the sides of the gym would break out their best (and probably most awkward) moves next, followed by the band and choir students who were sprinkled throughout the bleachers. *It's going to look pretty amazing*, she thought. Definitely a great way to end Spirit Week.

Jasmine plugged in the mic as everyone crowded into the gym. Teachers shushed students, trying to get everyone "under control." There was a brief pause. Then the pep band began to play. Cheerleaders flew through the air, flipping, clapping, cheering. The crowd was on their feet chanting their graduation years. Finally it was time. Jasmine stood up and walked to the center of the gym.

"I'm excited to introduce a man who is full of school spirit, Principal Mock!"

Jasmine handed the mic over to him. That was Eddy's cue. He turned on the music. Principal Mock started to dance, mechanically at first. As the other teachers joined the dancing, Principal Mock busted out his best Michael Jackson-esque moves. The dancing spread out from there just like the roar of the student body. The hard part was done. Now she just needed to fade in with all the other dancers in the bleachers.

She stepped into the bleachers toward Eddy. Something hit her, like a giant winter wind. It lifted her off her feet, but she did not fall on her face. The music kept blaring. Jasmine felt her whole body gripped by something cold as death. The icy wind flung her back and away from the bleachers, away from Eddy. She was a kite at the mercy of a hurricane—up and up she went, higher and higher. She was pinned, midair, in the center of the gym above the dancing principal who thought the increased cheering was because he had now started doing the "Gangnam Style" dance. Jasmine could do nothing. She just had time to catch her breath when the invisible power dragged her back to the opposite end of the gym.

The crowd went berserk. They leapt to their feet and clapped their hands. As far as the students were concerned, Jasmine had stolen the show, being carried up and over the gym by an invisible wire. But there was no invisible wire.

As the song faded, students and faculty surrounded Jasmine. They raved about the "special effects," about how real her "flying" routine looked—no visible cables or anything. They wouldn't stop bombarding her with compliments and questions. All the while not noticing Jasmine's posture: slumped, silent, and white as a ghost.

She tried to speak. "I-I-I didn't do anything. I d-d-don't know what happened. P-P-P-Please believe me." But no one did. In fact, they loved the whole spectacle even more. They thought it was all part of Jasmine's act, trying to make the stunt look like a supernatural event.

Only Mia and Hannah knew something was wrong. They pushed their way through the throng of people. Eddy was already next to her, whispering into her ear.

Before Hannah or Mia could stop him Eddy was lifting her from the chair saying, "I believe you. We have to get out of here. I can protect you."

All Jasmine wanted to do was leave, so she let Eddy scoop her up and carry her away.

Without Jasmine there the crowd quickly broke up. Teachers shooed students out the door or to their lockers. It was the end of the day and the end of a very long week. Students were happy to oblige. The homecoming football game was that evening with a dance to follow the next night.

Mia and Hannah slowly walked out the main doors of the school.

"We have to find her, Hannah."

CHAPTER 16

Mia and Hannah heard footsteps running up behind them. They turned to see Simon, to Hannah's disgust. They had known him since middle school. He had a gigantic crush on her.

"Hey ladies," Simon said. He was slightly out of breath

"Seriously, Simon. I'm not in the mood."

"No, I-I-I'm not going to ask you out, at least right now." He held out his phone. "You have to check this out. Jasmine, she's being lifted up. During the pep rally just now. It really wasn't just special effects! I got the whole thing on my phone."

They watched Jasmine get picked up by what could only be described as a shadow of a woman in a white dress.

"Did you see that! Did you see that! The lady in the dress." He was smiling from ear to ear.

"Rewind the clip, please," said Mia. At the bottom of the screen Hannah and Mia saw Eddy reaching for Jasmine as the shadow swept in between Eddy and Jasmine, forcing Jasmine away from Eddy.

"Oh, man, I can't wait to show everyone this." He sounded like he just won the lottery. "A ghost, a real genuine ghost. And she's hot! Of course, she's not as pretty as you, bae." Simon winked at Hannah.

"Simon!"

"Just saying!" Simon replied.

"Do you have a car here?" Hannah asked, ignoring him.

"Yeah."

"Can you give us a ride to the bog?"

"Heck no. I have big plans tonight, ladies!" He shoved his thick-rimmed glasses up his nose.

"Listen. I'll dance with you for one song at the homecoming dance this weekend if you just give us a ride out to the bog."

"Dance with me on *all* slow songs," Simon countered.

"Fine, but you have to erase the video, too," replied Hannah.

"Deal."

Hannah was already getting into his station wagon.

It was the longest five miles they had ever ridden. It was silent. Their minds raced. Even Simon could sense the gravity of the situation. The sun tucked itself behind some trees.

"I hope we aren't too late," said Mia as Simon parked the car.

The girls launched out of the doors and bolted to the bog's edge.

"I'll just wait here, ladies," Simon said nervously.

CHAPTER 17

Eddy stood on the edge of the bog with Jasmine. "I love you, Jasmine," he said, combing her hair with his fingers. "I only want you. Every night before the sun goes down I come back here and cross through the Gateway alone, but now we can cross together. Today is the first day of the rest of our lives." He chuckled as if he had just heard an inside joke, "Well, actually the first day of the rest of our deaths."

"What are you talking about?" asked Jasmine.

"At twilight I cross through the gateway into the land of the dead. That is where I belong now. If I don't return to where I belong my soul will die. Turn to dust." His eyes were wide. He put her hand to his heart. "In the past I wouldn't have really cared if I existed, but everything is different now. You are here."

Nothing. Jasmine felt no heartbeat, not even lungs that sucked in air.

"Last time, things went very wrong. Melanie fought me. I almost ran out of time, and she drowned." He gripped Jasmine's hand tighter. "I won't let that happen again."

"Ow, you're hurting me."

"Oh darling, you won't have to feel pain ever again." He pulled Jasmine into the bog. "Quickly, the sun is almost down."

"Stop! What are you doing?" Jasmine was up to her chest in the cold sludge of the bog.

"I love you so much. More than I ever loved Melanie." He pressed her head underwater. "I know this doesn't make any sense now, but soon it will."

Jasmine was spitting and sputtering.

"You and I can be together forever."

Mud was in her mouth and up her nose. Jasmine tried to fight him. She tried to swing behind and kick and flail, but he was too strong. Her whole body went limp. The bog's darkness was swallowing her. Things went black. She could feel her body sinking into the greasy mud.

Suddenly there was a tug on Jasmine's arm. Pulling her back. Back to air. Back to breathing. Back to life.

It was Mia.

Next to her, Hannah held a huge rock. She was hitting Eddy over the head over and over again, knocking him down just long enough for Mia and Jasmine to run to shore.

Eddy pulled himself back up to his feet. He ran after Jasmine and Mia.

The sun was just a sliver on the horizon.

Grabbing Jasmine's ankle, Eddy dragged her back to the bog. Mia, and now Hannah too, pulled Jasmine's arms, trying desperately to free her from his murderous grip. He was too strong.

"I will never let you go." His voice was calm, certain. "I told you: you are mine for—"

The sun finally dipped beneath the horizon.

Eddy's flesh collapsed around his bones, starting with his face, moving down his shoulders to his spindly fingers. He was skin on bone. Bones dried and splintered. Jasmine, Mia, and Hannah watched a man go from youth to dead to decomposed to dust. Like an autumn leaf, the wind took what was left of Eddy and scattered it across the bog. All that was left was his pocket watch. It lay where his body once did.

The girls huddled together, cold and wet but alive. And friends. They had never been so grateful to have each other.

They tromped back to Simon's wagon. And like a gentleman, Simon unlocked the doors and handed a box of Kleenex to the three girls.

"You have a little something on your—" Simon waved his hand all around his face and chest. "Well, pretty much everywhere."

It was true. They were all covered in bog slime.

It started with Jasmine—a contagious giggle. Then Hannah caught it, and Mia too. Soon all three of them were laughing and couldn't stop. "I guess this is better than crying," said Jasmine. "That is absolutely the most terrifying thing that I have ever been through. You guys, I was sure—*sure*—that I was going to die."

"You're OK now," Mia said. "We've got you. Three strong women have got to stick together."

"No matter what," said Hannah. "Say, Jasmine, I love your new eye shadow. Can I borrow some?"

Jasmine wiped some of the muck off her forehead and smeared it across Hannah's eyebrow.

"Thanks!" Hannah said.

They started laughing all over again.

"So are you going to shower before the dance tomorrow night?" Simon said all of a sudden.

For a few moments, they'd forgotten he was there.

"About that dance . . ." Hannah said. "I . . . I've kind of been through a lot tonight, Simon. I know I promised, but . . . I'm just not sure now that I can go."

"Yeah, I figured it was too good to be true," Simon said, sounding totally unfazed by the rejection. "C'mon. I'll give you a ride home."

They climbed in the car.

When they arrived at Mia's house, all three girls got out.

"Will you do me a favor?" Simon said, his window rolled down. "Will you say hi to me in the halls every once in a while?"

"Of course, Simon." Hannah leaned over and gave him a tiny, muddy peck on the cheek.

He made a noise that sounded an awful lot like a squeal. "Does this mean—"

"No!" all of the girls replied.

CHAPTER 18

In the days that followed, Jasmine gave the earring to the police along with the pocket watch. The police were able to link Edmund Trefare, the jeweler's son, to Melanie Zurner's death. A two-hundred-year-old murder case was finally solved. And Mia, Hannah, and Jasmine were to thank.

"You know, I think the police department would really benefit from our detective services," said Hannah. She and her two best friends biked back to the bog for one last visit before winter.

"Just as long as the cases don't involve slimy dead things," Mia said.

"Or ghosts," said Jasmine.

They parked their bikes and walked to the bog. Stillness lingered, but not the creepy kind they had felt weeks ago.

Tiny white flowers covered the velvety moss on the bog. Mia, Hannah, and Jasmine sat on a nearby log. Mourning doves cooed before the sun completely set. In the distance they saw her—Melanie Zurner. Her almost-invisible outline turned to them and waved good-bye. She faded into the bog's mist.

"It's crazy to think of where all this began," said Hannah.

"*The Atlas of Cursed Places*," said Jasmine.

"Actually, no. It all started with Mia and a little butterfly clip of Grammy's."

Mia was silent. She could feel tears coming. "I'm glad I didn't see Grammy. She wouldn't have been the same as I remembered." Then she paused. "I do kind of wish I knew if she was okay."

A gentle breeze touched their faces as a butterfly landed right on Mia's shoulder. It stayed there looking at her, moving its delicate wings as if to say "Hello." On the next gentle breeze it lifted and flew into the setting sun.

CASE 1:
THE HAUNTING OF APARTMENT 101

Jinx was a social reject who became a punked-out paranormal investigator. Jackson is a jock by day and Jinx's ghost-hunting partner by night. When a popular girl named Emily asks the duo to explore a haunting in her dad's apartment, Jinx is skeptical—but Jackson insists they take the case. And the truth they find is even stranger than Emily's story.

CASE 2:
THE TERROR OF BLACK EAGLE TAVERN

Jinx's ghost-hunting partner Jackson may be a jock, but Jinx is not interested in helping his football buddy Todd—until Todd's case gets too weird to ignore. A supernatural presence is causing chaos at the bar Todd's family owns. And the threat has a connection to Todd that's deeper than even he realizes . . .

CASE 3:
THE MAYHEM ON MOHAWK AVENUE

Jinx and Jackson have become the go-to ghost hunters at their high school. When a new kid in town tries to get in on their business, Jinx is furious. Portland only needs one team to track down ghosties! But Jinx's quest to shut down her competition will lead her and Jackson down a dangerous path . . .

CASE 4:
THE BRIDGE OF DEATH

Jinx is the top paranormal investigator at her high school, and she has a blog to prove it. Jackson's her ghost-hunting partner by night—former partner, anyway. After a shakeup in the Paranormalists' operation, the two ex–best friends are on the outs, and at the worst possible time. Because a deadly supernatural threat is putting their classmates in harm's way . . .

ABOUT THE AUTHOR

Kathryn J. Beherns has a Master's of Fine Arts in Writing for Children and Young Adults and an undergraduate degree in English Education with a decade of experience teaching young writers. She has also taught writing classes for teens at the Loft Literary Center and is currently an adjunct English instructor. She believes reading and writing connect people to everything else and that words (written, read, spoken, screamed, sung, whispered, shared) make us more alive!